UNEXPECTED

J.M. GOODRICH

Unexpected

J.M. Goodrich

ALSO BY J.M. GOODRICH

Deadly Celebrations

Emily's Wish

Snowflakes & Heartaches

Undying Love

Coming Home

Love Me Right

Summer Nights

Spirit And Soul

Bruised Heart

Just One Night

After All This Time

To Be Loved

Last Resort

UNEXPECTED

Sophie's world has been turned upside down when she found out she was pregnant.
And then tragedy strikes and she finds herself alone.
It seems that the hits just keep on coming.

But then in walks Tripp, her knight in shining armor.
Tripp was someone she hadn't seen since their high school years together.
Her old crush.
Her first crush.
And now the man who will piece together her broken heart, and teach her that it's okay to love again.
Together, they navigate life, conquering the new challenges they face as they prepare to welcome her little one into the world.
Even through tragedy and heartache, love will prevail.

CHAPTER 1

ophie

I STARED down at the two little plastic sticks sitting on the edge of my bathroom sink.

This can't be real.

But it is.

The first one, had two little pink lines that seemed to be staring right back at me. The other had just one word - pregnant.

How did this happen?

I mean, I know how.

But *how?*

I had no idea how Ryan, my boyfriend, was going to feel about this new, little development.

Let's face it, I had no idea how I even felt about it.

I've always wanted children. But not now.

Later.

Much later.

I still had so much that I wanted to accomplish first. I had dreams. Goals. Now all of that would have to be pushed to the side.

Ryan and I weren't even engaged yet. We have never had any discussions about rings or dresses or venues. We just loved each other and wanted to be together. That was enough for us at the moment.

Or at least it was.

Now . . .

Now I have no idea.

Would he be happy about this?

Angry?

Would he break up with me over this?

There were so many possibilities. Most of which could hurt me. And that fact scares me. I love Ryan so much. I couldn't lose him. I don't know what I would do without him.

I knew I had to tell him though. I had no choice.

I just don't *want* to.

Deciding to just get it over with, I grabbed the tests, carefully putting them in a little plastic bag, and shoved them in my purse. I wasn't sure if I'd just hand them to Ryan, letting him come to his own conclusion, or what I would even say to him. But if I didn't go to him now, who knows how long I'd stall the news.

We would figure this out together.

My feet were heavy as I lifted them to walk up the stairs to Ryan's floor. Why couldn't this building have an elevator?

When I finally reached his floor I slowly began making my way down the hall to his door. I was so nervous I felt nauseous. Or then again it could be something else.

Because I'm pregnant.

To be honest, we haven't talked about this. At all. Not one conversation about having children. We hadn't been dating all that long, just a couple years. We haven't even moved in together yet. We each still had a little over a year left before graduating college, so we had agreed to live apart until after graduation to give each of us the space and time to focus on our studies, get our degrees.

Then our life together could truly begin. There would be nothing left standing in the way.

I stopped, looking down at my stomach. *Except for this*, I thought, rubbing my hand over the tiny bump that had already begun to form.

I reached his door yet hesitated, still unsure of what exactly I was going to say to him. I just knew I had to tell him.

Tell him that everything was changing. All the plans we had, all our hopes for the future. Everything.

Nothing would ever be the same.

I raised my hand to knock, but paused mid air. I heard voices.

Several voices seemed to be coming from his apartment. Most of them are female.

Now I really felt sick.

I debated turning around and going home. I could confront him about this later, when I've calmed down. Then I could tell him my news.

My nerves were already shot, with finding out I was expecting a child, but now to come to my boyfriend's apartment and hear it filled with other women? I don't know if my heart could take his explanation.

I looked back down the long hallway. I really didn't want to go all the way home right now. I didn't want to be alone. Besides, I should tell him the news. He deserves to know. I did come all this way to tell him after all.

And I did not want to have to make this trip again. I would absolutely lose my nerve if I left.

So I sucked in a deep breath and knocked on the door.

It swung open to reveal Ryan's mother. She was clutching a handkerchief to her chest, her eyes red rimmed and puffy.

"Sophie! Oh, I'm so glad you made it," she cried, pulling me into a tight hug. Over her shoulder I could see the rest of Ryan's family, along with a few others I haven't met.

It gave me an uneasy feeling.

What was going on?

"Where's Ryan?" I asked, wriggling out of his mother's grasp. "I really need to speak with him. It's important."

Away from all these people. I had no intention of springing the news on him in front of his entire family.

She looked at me with a mixture of confusion and sadness in her eyes. "He's gone," she says in a tone that implies that I'm an idiot for even asking. She loudly blew her nose, fresh tears finding their way down her face.

I looked around to everyone else, who had stopped what they were doing to watch our interaction. Maria, one of his sisters, was looking at me wide eyed. She stepped up to her mother, placing a hand softly on her arm. "I don't think she knows," she whispered sadly.

The feeling of unease intensified.

Her mother looked directly at me, her eyes searching mine. I was feeling more nervous, more nauseous as the seconds ticked by.

Without a word I was ushered to the couch and then told to sit down. Everyone gathered around as Mrs Fields sat down next to me. She grabbed my hands, holding them tight as she spoke the words that would shatter my entire world.

Ryan's dead.

"He was out riding his motorcycle last night. He took a corner a little too fast," she explained, her breath coming fast and her voice trembling. "He never made it. They didn't find his body until this morning."

His body. My heart stopped beating with those words. How could this be true? We just had dinner together last night. Nothing was out of the ordinary. Nothing to indicate that it would be the last time we would ever get to spend together. Everything was fine. We were both so in love, so happy.

Everything was perfect.

I refuse to accept this. I refuse to accept that the love of my life was taken from me with no warning whatsoever.

I hated that damn motorcycle. I always had. It always gave me a bad feeling.

I didn't hear anything else that anyone said after that. All I remember were the tears, and everyone hugging me. I didn't want to be touched. I didn't want to be here. I wanted to be alone.

Just me and my heartache.

I finally excused myself after about an hour and made my way home. I closed the door, setting my purse and keys on the entryway table. This place felt empty, more than usual. I lived alone, but this time . . . it was different.

I took about two steps into the living room before sinking to the floor in a puddle of grief. How could this have happened? Ryan didn't deserve this.

I didn't deserve this.

As I cried on the floor I rubbed my non-existent belly.

Our baby certainly didn't deserve this. He or she would never get to know their father.

And Ryan would never know that he was about to be one.

CHAPTER 2

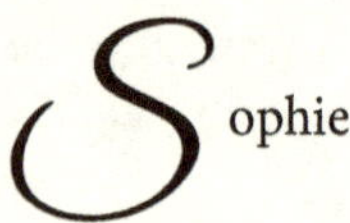ophie

I RUBBED my three month belly, if you could even call it that. It was more of a small bump, if anything. Barely visible. Still, it amazed me. Everything about being pregnant has so far. I've always heard horror stories, but so far I feel I've been quite lucky.

I was, of course, if you didn't count the fact that I lost the baby's father.

While I was finally starting to get excited at the thought of having a mini-me or mini-Ryan around, I was even more sad that neither one will know the other. It's not fair that Ryan never even had the chance to know he was going to be a father.

He was always so loving and caring. And I know he would have been the best dad ever to our little one.

That's the absolute hardest thing about this entire situation.

Looking around my crappy apartment, I realized two things.

One - I'd have to try to move, there was no room here to comfortably raise a baby.

And two - I needed to begin looking for and purchasing some baby items. Sure, I have a few months still before the baby's arrival to prepare, but at the same time, I didn't have a single thing for him or her.

I grabbed my purse, slipping on my shoes. I decided to at least window shop today, to begin gathering ideas for what I would need and want. Plus, I could really use the exercise. I hadn't done much besides sit around and mourn Ryan. It wasn't healthy for me or the little one.

I wasn't prepared for how emotional just holding a tiny sock would make me. Or teeny tiny pants and dresses. They were just so damn cute. I couldn't wait to dress up my little one in all sorts of tiny outfits.

I was looking in the window of a shop that was way too expensive for me to even step foot in when I heard a voice that sounded familiar, although I couldn't quite place it.

"Sophie?"

I turned towards the man who had called my name, my heart stopping the second my eyes landed on his handsome and familiar face.

Tripp Lawson.

We attended the same high school together when we were younger. Though we never really spoke. We hung out with completely different friend circles. I absolutely knew who he was though because I had the biggest crush on him all throughout school. Because of this I was too shy to even go up and introduce myself to him. But I remembered who he was, as he had crept into my mind every few months.

I hadn't seen him since our school years, and here he was, standing right in front of me. He was wearing a business suit, which hung perfectly on his broad shoulders. He looked good.

Really good.

I shook my head, realizing I had been staring. "Tripp?" I asked, even though I was sure it was him.

He nodded, smiling wide. "So it is you," he said, a smile forming on his lips.

His full, oh-so-kissable lips.

I smiled back, not knowing what to say. It felt like I was in high school all over again, with the shyness taking over me. I looked to the ground, feeling the heat creeping up the back of my neck.

Tripp let out a small, nervous sigh.

Somehow, it was comforting to know he was just as confident as I felt.

"So how have you been?" he asked, breaking the silence. "How has life been treating you?"

"Not as well as I had hoped," I scoffed.

His eyes flickered down to my barely-there bump and then back up to my eyes.

"God, I'm sorry," I said, clearing my throat.

Tripp put his hands up. "It's alright. I did ask."

I took a deep breath. "It just hasn't been the best few weeks, if I'm being completely honest."

He nodded, a sympathetic look on his face. I hated when people looked at me like that. Like they pitied me.

The poor single mom.

Even though he didn't know that little tidbit yet.

"Well, how about you tell me about it over coffee," he suggested. I scrunched up my face.

"Or juice or soda," he laughed. "You don't even have to tell me what happened if you don't want to. We could just grab a snack and catch up a bit. It's been years."

Right on cue my stomach growled. It would be nice to

talk to and spend some time with Tripp. Besides, I've been walking around town for a while, my feet were killing me. So I agreed and he led me to a nearby cafe that had the most amazing sandwiches.

As we ate we fell into a comfortable rhythm of asking each other questions about our lives since high school, getting to know each other all over again. For the first time in weeks, I actually began to enjoy myself.

I still had times where I felt guilty any time I had even the smallest moment of happiness. It felt like I wasn't allowed to smile and enjoy life.

Not when the man I loved wasn't here.

A part of me felt horrible any time Tripp made me laugh or feel good. I felt as though laughing with another man, especially so soon, was somehow a betrayal to Ryan and his memory.

As if he didn't matter that much to me.

I know I wasn't doing anything to tarnish his memory.

I did nothing wrong.

So why does it feel like it?

"So," Tripp cleared his throat, stealing back my attention, "where's your mind at right now?"

I felt my cheeks heat with embarrassment. I didn't want to confess that I had been thinking about another man.

Although, I suppose it was okay that the other man was the father of my unborn child.

Still.

"I'm sorry. I realize I haven't been the best lunch companion." I let out a long breath. "There just always seems to be a lot on my mind lately."

Tripp nodded in understanding. "You know you can tell me anything," he offered, his voice low and comforting.

So comforting, in fact, that the next thing I knew, the words just poured out of me. I unleashed my sad tale from the past few weeks on poor Tripp. The entire time he just sat quietly, hanging onto my every word.

He reached across the table, gently taking my hand in his. "I am so sorry for what you have gone through. I can't imagine how you must be feeling. I know for now we're still practically strangers, but if you ever need anything, don't hesitate to reach out to me. I'll be there for you in a heartbeat."

The sincerity in his eyes made me melt a little. "Thank you," I told him. "I really appreciate it."

"Anytime," he smiled.

I didn't know if I'd ever actually take him up on the offer, but I loved knowing that there was at least someone in my corner if I needed them.

CHAPTER 3

ophie

I DON'T RECOMMEND MISSING work. Not any more than absolutely necessary, anyway. After Ryan's death I became depressed. I didn't eat. I didn't sleep. I hardly left the house, while refusing to answer any calls or texts.

I just wanted to be left alone.

Because of all of this, I skipped out on work, causing me to end up being fired. It wasn't the best job in the world, I'll admit that. I worked at a local clothing store, but still, it was a job. It had provided me, even though barely, with enough money for rent, food, and my phone bill.

Now, I have no job. And because of this, I wasn't able to pay rent. So now I have no home. Well, I have until next month until I absolutely have to be out of here, but still. I didn't know what I was going to do. How was I supposed to find a new place to live within a month? And with no job to boot

I tried not to panic as I ran around town applying to wherever I could. After a little over a week of doing this with no luck, I began to feel hopeless. After putting in each application I did follow up with a call to check up on them, but no one seemed to want to hire a pregnant woman. I mean, I *kinda* get it, but that doesn't make that fact suck any less.

I was about to give up, but told myself, "One more. Just one more application for today." Then I could go home, rest up, and come up with a new plan. Obviously what I'm doing now isn't working.

Looking to my left, I noticed a building I can't recall ever seeing. Not that I paid attention to each and every building in the city. It had a big shiny logo on the front that said 'TL Inc' on it. The name meant nothing to me, yet something told me that I should try my luck there. I shrugged, figuring it couldn't hurt.

Stepping through the front door, I immediately felt out of place. Young, polished, professional looking men and women were everywhere. High heels clicked as the women walked across the floor. Men adjusted their ties as they chatted away on their cell phones that probably cost more than what I paid monthly in rent.

My face burned with embarrassment as I looked down at my own outfit. I had on a pair of black dress slacks that I had purchased years ago. With the pregnancy this would be one of the last times I'd be able to wear them for a while. Paired with them I wore a plain white, flowy peasant top. It was simple, but I figured the black and white look was somewhat professional looking, even if just on the lower end of the scale. On the plus side, the top hid my stomach a bit. I'm sure some women figured that fact out on their own, because women knew women. Intuition and all that. But mostly I decided to just come right out and be completely honest that I was expecting. Which turned out to not work in my favor.

But what could I do? It was better than lying and then having to do this all over again.

Gathering up every last shred of courage, I walked up to the front desk. The woman seated behind it didn't even look up from her phone. I cleared my throat. "Excuse me."

That finally got her attention. She looked up and down, slowly raking her eyes over me with disgust clearly written all over her face. "Yes?" She asked, turning her attention back to her phone.

Clearly, helping clients and potential new employees is a huge priority to this woman.

I shifted from one foot to the other, beginning to feel a little embarrassed about even stepping foot in here. "I . . . I came here to put in an application, in case there were any job openings." I stuttered, hating myself immediately afterwards. I had worked on what to say to potential employers all week, so I could sound somewhat professional and avoid interactions like this. Instead, I came off as a teen applying for their very first job ever.

I set my resume on her desk.

The woman looked from it to me, then scoffed. "*You* want to apply *here*?" She asked, voice dripping with condescension. "What could you possibly be qualified to do?" A smirk spread across her face.

I could ask her the same question.

"Cassie!" A man yelled nearby, startling us both. turned to look at whoever just yelled and my heart stopped.

Tripp freaking Lawson.

Of course.

He was staring at Cassie, eyes burning in anger. "We have talked about this before. Is that any way to speak to our clients?"

Cassie just rolled her eyes, plopping herself down in her desk chair with a huff.

That's when Tripp finally noticed that it was me who was the recipient of Cassie's friendly behavior. His face softened, his anger evaporating.

"Sophie? What a pleasant surprise. What are you doing here?" His eyes filled with hope. I briefly wondered if he thought I had sought him out, and that was the purpose of my visit.

My eyes flicked to Cassie real quick, who was now hunched down in her chair, trying to hide from Tripp's anger.

Did he work here? Was he her boss?

That possibility ignited a small spark of hope within me. I know it might be wrong, but perhaps he might be able to put in a good word for me with whoever did the hiring.

I move my gaze back to my old friend, happier than ever that we had recently reunited. I stand a little straighter, to hopefully convince Tripp that Cassie hadn't affected me even a little bit.

"I just came by to inquire about a possible job opening." I told him with the confidence I had lacked a minute ago.

Tripp raised an eyebrow at me. "You mean you're not here just to pay me a visit?" he pouted, a smile playing on his lips.

His soft, oh-so-kissable lips.

Seriously, when did he grow up to be *this*? I'll admit that I barely noticed him during school. Which sounds awful, I know. But back then I hardly noticed any guy, no matter how attractive they happened to be. I focused all my time and energy on studying and getting good grades. That was the only thing that was important to me then.

Yeah, and look where that got me.

I smiled shyly at Tripp, my face ablaze.

"Why don't you come on up to my office," he said. He gestured for me to follow him, then, turning back to Cassie, pointed a finger at her. "You and I will talk later," he told her, voice edged with warning. Cassie looked close to tears.

Not so tough now, huh?

I silently got into the elevator with Tripp, following him to his office.

I had a feeling that my day was about to turn around.

CHAPTER 4

ripp

I MAY BE GETTING AHEAD of myself here, but this feels as if it may be fate.

Even if she is carrying another man's child.

It doesn't affect my feelings towards her one bit. I still want her just as much as ever.

And as for her unborn child, I could love it as my own. I *would* love it as my own, I have absolutely no doubt about that. I've loved their mother for years, albeit from afar. I would certainly love a little baby that was a part of her.

How could I not?

Now here she was, sitting across from me in my office. We hadn't seen each other in years, yet she had always been on my mind. When we met I was shy and awkward. No matter how big my crush on her may have been, I never would have had the courage to go up to her and so much as introduce myself.

But times have changed. I'm no longer the timid young teen that I once was. I feel like in a twisted way I have been handed a second chance. And I'm sure as hell going to take it.

I'm going to take things slow, don't get me wrong. But I absolutely cannot let this chance pass me by.

It could be my last.

She sat across from me, looking nervous as hell. It was adorable. She had nothing to worry about though. After running into her and catching up I did some checking up on her. Nothing major or creepy, just to see how she was doing in life and her qualifications and all that. I already knew I would be offering her a job by the end of this meeting.

I'd be lying If I said I wasn't excited about the possibility of working with her and getting to have her near me all the time.

With time, I hope it will bring us closer.

Sophie began nervously explaining her experience and qualifications, how she hoped to, and was willing to learn and grow within the company. I'll admit, I only half listened to anything she was saying, as my mind began to wander.

I promise, I'm usually much more professional than this.

But Sophie just does something to me. Something I can't quite put my finger on. Right now, even though it's all I should be interested in hearing about, I didn't want to know all about her background, her past jobs. I knew about that already.

I wanted to know about *her*, about the woman she's become. Her likes, dislikes. Does she have any hobbies? What are her dreams?

What would her lips feel like pressed against mine?

". . . and that's why I feel I may be a great asset here at TL Inc," she said, a slight shake in her voice.

Her words brought me out of my increasingly inappropriate daydreams. I cleared my throat, blinking a few times to bring myself back to the present.

"I agree," I told her, looking her straight in the eye. I realized I hadn't heard a single word she had said. But what did that matter, really, when I knew she would be hired the moment I saw her walk into my building and offer her resume at the front desk.

Sophie looked back at me, eyes wide. The look on her face told me she didn't believe the words that I had just told her. I cleared my throat to cover up my small laugh. This woman was absolutely adorable.

"You . . ."

"I agree," I told her again. "You're going to be an amazing addition to our team."

"You mean I . . ."

"Got the job, yes." I nodded.

She let out a small laugh of disbelief, sitting back in her chair. She took a few seconds to process everything and compose herself. "Thank you," she said, her voice a little shaky. "I promise you won't regret this decision. I'll work hard and make you proud."

I smiled at that. I had no doubt that she would.

She then quickly cleared her throat. "I mean, I'll . . . I'll make the company proud."

I watched as her face grew different shades of red. It made me wonder if it was her words or was it me that made her nervous.

Perhaps I was foolish in thinking that she could maybe want me too. But after reconnecting with her, there was just something telling me that I couldn't let her go. I couldn't let her slip away this time.

Not without a fight.

I was a kid back then, barely even knowing what love was. But this time around it was different. We were both adults. Although the situation wasn't ideal, it was nothing I couldn't handle. It didn't change the fact that she was still the amazing woman I had fallen for all those years ago.

I stood up, determination coursing through me. "Let me show you around," I offered, extending my hand.

I showed her around the office, giving her the most thorough tour I ever have, in order to drag out our time together. I knew I would be seeing her more often given we now work at the same place, but I still wanted to spend as much time as I could with her at this moment.

After showing her around every inch of the office, I realized our time together for now was quickly coming to a close.

But there was one more thing I could still show her.

Her new position.

"Now, if you'll follow me one more time, I will show you where you'll be working."

"Awesome," she said excitedly, clapping her hands together. I had to turn my head a little to hide my laughter.

We stepped into the elevator and rode back down to the first floor. On the way, I filled her in on everything her job would entail.

"Now, I hope you don't take this the wrong way," I began, noticing her shift with a sudden unease, "but I figured with your pregnancy, we would start you off with an easier position."

I swear I saw a flash of panic in her eyes.

I held up my hands. "It's not to say I doubt your abilities. At all," I quickly reassured her. "I know you'll do a fantastic job no matter where you are in the company. But we'll start you off at the front desk. And then after you give birth and are all settled, we'll talk about where to go next. Something much more challenging."

Sophie stared at the elevator door, and I feared she might

be rethinking her employment here. Not that I could really blame her. I could have worded things better. I just get so tongue-tied around her.

She turned to me after a few more seconds of uncomfortable silence. "I think that's a great idea," she finally said. "I suppose it would be easier to learn a more challenging job when I have the time and headspace to actually focus. I appreciate you for thinking of me like that. Thank you." She smiled genuinely at me.

I let out a sigh of relief.

The elevator came to a stop and we stepped out. I led her back to the front desk where we first met this morning.

Placing my hand on the desk, I suddenly wished that I had done this earlier. Firing Cassie has been a long time coming.

A *long* time coming.

But still, I should have met with her while Sophie was in the bathroom or something.

I should have thought this through. The last thing I wanted was to look like a jerk in her eyes.

"Cassie . . ." I began. Sophie let out a gasp.

Shit.

I knew I should have waited. I did not want to start our working relationship out on the wrong foot. I wanted her to like me, not the complete opposite.

"I completely forgot, I have a doctor's appointment," she said, eyes wide. "I have to go, I'm so sorry." She turned to run towards the door, then stopped, looking back at me. "Thank you so much for this opportunity Tripp, you have no idea how much I appreciate it. I promise, I won't let you down. And I'm so sorry that I have to go."

I waved her off. "No worries. We can talk about the details later. And if you hang on for just a second, I'll have my driver take you to your appointment." I pressed a number on my cell, summoning my driver.

I'll give him a big fate tip for this.

"Oh, that's not necessary," she began to protest. But again, I waved her off. I knew she didn't own a car. She had mentioned it at our lunch the other day.

"He's already outside, waiting," I told her. She thanked me profusely and left.

I watched until the cat was out of sight, then turned my attention to Cassie, seated behind the desk. She was fiddling with her phone without a care in the world, as if the company owner wasn't standing directly in front of her.

I loudly cleared my throat, thinking that would get her attention and make her at least put her phone away.

Nope.

Instead, she barely even glanced my way.

"Can I help you?" She asked, voice dripping with annoyance.

Now, I am beginning to get angry. I have given this girl countless chances to straighten up her act and grow up. Show at least a little bit of professionalism.

"Cassie," I bellowed. "You need to pack up your things."

She shot out of her chair.

At least that caught her attention.

"What do you mean?" She whined. "Why?"

I crossed my arms over my chest. "I think you know why."

Cassie scoffed, rolling her eyes. "I'm fired, aren't I?"

How fast she changes her attitude is a little unnerving.

"Yes, Cassie. You're fired."

"Whatever," she rolled her eyes again. She took her time grabbing her things and then walked out of the building without a single glance back.

How I put up with her for this long was beyond me.

Looking at her vacant seat, I began to feel better. Not

only was I certain that Sophie would do a much better job, hell, I mean, my left shoe could do a better job than Cassie, but Sophie's gorgeous face would be the first thing I saw every morning when I walked into the building.

My life just got a little bit better.

CHAPTER 5

ophie

THE PAST COUPLE of months have been an absolute whirlwind. Between learning the ropes at my new job, doctor visits, and everything else concerning the baby, I've been nothing but busy.

All day.

Every day.

To top it off, Tripp and I have become a lot closer. So close, in fact, that we have decided to give a relationship between us a shot. It's been amazing so far. Better than I thought it would be, actually. We decided that with the baby and everything, that we would be together, but we would take things slow.

Well, except for one thing.

We moved in together.

More specifically, I moved in with Tripp into his place. It took him a lot to convince me, even though I desperately needed a place to stay. I had been staying in a hotel after leaving my last apartment.

And really, I had nowhere else to go.

We had just started dating, it was way too soon to cohabitate. But Tripp had insisted, saying it would be easier for him to take care of both me and the baby.

I'll admit, I cried like a baby when he said that.

I blame the hormones.

But honestly, I was grateful for Tripp, and everything that he was doing for me. There was nothing I could have done to deserve any of this.

Tripp took my bags from me. "While you're staying here, don't think of me as your boss. Think of me as the same guy you've known from high school," he said.

"But I didn't really know you in high school," I pointed out.

"True," he clicked his tongue. "Then how about a friend? New friend," he laughed.

I loved the sound. He suddenly stopped. "I guess we're more than friends now, though."

Which was true. We had agreed to give us a chance, taking it slow, considering the circumstances.

His smile stayed in place. "Follow me," he gestured, leading me through his house to the spare bedroom. He gave me a mini tour along the way.

I couldn't help but get stuck on the fact that his spare bedroom was directly next to his own.

It was comforting, in case anything happened with the baby. But at the same time it made me nervous, having Tripp so close. This man had always done something to me, but it's always been from afar. We always had a distance between us.

Now, the distance has been reduced to a single wall.

How was I supposed to get any rest knowing he was just on the other side of it?

And with that several dark, dirty thoughts entered my head. Thoughts that had no business even being there in the first place. I tried to push those thoughts away. No matter what I wanted, I had to be careful. He wasn't just myself that I had to think about now.

Tripp and I had promised to take things slow, what, with the baby and all. While I respected Tripp's decision, loving the fact that he was respectful and looking out for me, my body wanted other things. I had no idea if it was the pregnancy hormones or what, but my attraction to him was in overdrive. It was sometimes hard to keep it together just standing next to the man.

And now I was living with him. I've never lived with a man before, so this was all completely new to me. In fact, I've never even had a roommate before.

As soon as I was able to, I moved out of my parents house and into my own place.

Alone.

I loved my privacy. I loved having my own space.

Not having to answer to anyone.

I was ashamed to admit I didn't know the first thing about living with a guy as an adult. Did I have to ask permission to use things like the stove or microwave everytime? Let him know every time I left the house, where I was going and who I was with? I wasn't sure.

But as it would turn out I wouldn't need to worry about any of that. Not only did Tripp have chefs and maids employed, but he was an amazing cook himself.

And he never let me lift a finger around the house. I was always told to rest and put up my feet, while Tripp took care of whatever it was or brought me a delicious green smoothie.

To be honest, I wasn't sure if this was something I could get used to. All my life I have done everything myself. I've known nothing but independence.

I did enjoy being around Tripp though.

This man . . . the more I got to know him and was around him . . . the more I *wanted* to be around him.

He was everything I didn't know I needed.

Ryan had loved and cared for me deeply, don't get me wrong.

But Tripp . . .

Tripp absolutely pampered my ass and catered to my every need. He was loving and attentive, always hanging onto my every word when I spoke.

I didn't deserve this man.

But I was eternally grateful for him.

I'm aware of just how lucky I was to even have him in my life.

And I vow to do everything within my power to show him just how I feel.

CHAPTER 6

ophie

"WE MAY NOW HAVE RUN in the same circles, but even then, I knew you were the one I was going to end up with."

"Seriously?"

He nodded. "Within the first few minutes of seeing you. I just had that feeling," he shrugged. "And it never left."

My heart jumped in my chest. All this time he felt about me the exact same way I had felt about him? My mind raced with possibilities, like what we could have been.

Or still be.

Although, who knows what or where life would have brought us. If we had gotten together back in high school, chances are we would have just dated for a few weeks and then parted ways. It was a rare thing for high school loves to work out.

Everybody knows that.

And I would have hated it if Tripp and I had dated and ended on bad terms.

If the two of us hated each other now.

I'm devastated just at the thought of it. I try to put those thoughts away, and face the amazing present we are having together.

And the even more amazing future we're going to have.

Admittedly, I've never thought about Tripp as being fatherly before.

Hell, I've never thought of myself as motherly.

Yet here we are.

But these past couple months together has changed all that. The baby's not even here, yet he's already been so caring and attentive.

I swear, the man has read every single book on parenting that has ever been written. It warmed my heart every time I saw him poring over one of those books.

I'm pretty sure he's even more prepared than I am at this point for the baby's arrival.

Usually, I'm pretty good with being organized and making sure I'm prepared for whatever is needed. But ever since Ryan's passing, my mind has constantly been racing. It feels as though I'll never get my life settled back down, and in a constant state of worry and anxiety.

It's beyond frustrating.

I know I should be preparing for this baby and working on getting my life together, but lately it's been an impossible feeling.

How can I pick baby names and put together a nursery when I feel like I'm continuously drowning? It's hard to breathe most days and my head is swimming.

There's no end in sight.

No relief.

No sign that I can soon come up for air and breathe.

Tripp has been trying his best to help me though. Honestly, without him I wouldn't have been able to claw my way out of this hole as much as I had.

I owe him a lot.

A lot more than I was sure I'd be able to repay him.

But I will try my hardest.

Not just for Tripp, but also for my little one.

For my family.

It almost felt weird to think that a couple months ago, it seemed like I had nothing. That I had lost everything.

Now I have a family.

I would always miss Ryan, and a part of him will always be with me. Especially within his son or daughter. Thankfully, Tripp knew and understood this. He didn't seem like the jealous type, which I also appreciate.

I couldn't wait to build this family with him.

CHAPTER 7

ophie

I. Aᴍ. Exhausted.

Tripp had woken me up very early this morning, and then sent me on a bunch of errands. He said that they were very important and absolutely had to be done today, so I didn't really have a choice.

Rude.

And of course he had a couple of important meetings to go to today, meaning he wouldn't be able to go with me. And I'd have to go alone.

This sucks. Dragging my heavily pregnant self all over town is the complete opposite of a good time.

Most of the errands had to do with the baby, so I begrudgingly agreed to go. I was kicking myself for leaving so much til the last second.

I just wanted Tripp here to help me. Plus, I just loved being around him.

After running around the entire day, gathering the necessary items needed to finish preparing for our little one's arrival, I was ready to go home and put my aching feet up. Maybe I could even convince Tripp to give me a foot rub.

Walking through the front door, I set all my purchases down in the living room. I went over the list Tripp had given me, making sure I had finished each and every one. I did not want to have to go back out there again.

As soon as I plopped myself down on the couch, Tripp walked out from the bedrooms, startling me.

"I thought you were working," I said, placing a hand on my chest to steady my heartbeat. "You scared me."

Tripp chuckled, leaning down to give me a quick kiss. "I am working," he smiled reassuringly.

"If you were going to be home, you should have just come out and helped me." I playfully slapped his arm. "That was not nice of you to make big fat pregnant me do everything myself." I put on my best pouty face.

"You are adorable," he said, kissing the top of my head. "And I promise you, I've been very busy. And I can't wait for you to see what I've done."

He laughed when I raised an eyebrow at him.

Tripp held out a hand, his eyes twinkling. "Follow me."

You don't have to tell me twice.

I obeyed, and when we were close to my bedroom, he slipped a hand over my eyes.

"It's a surprise," he whispered, his breath warm against my ear.

After an uncomfortable few seconds, he stopped us. "Ready?"

I nodded.

He released his hand. I blinked a few times, bringing everything into focus.

We were standing inside my bathroom.

That had completely changed.

I looked around the room, which now included a brand new vanity sink, enlarged shower, and my absolute favorite new feature - a jacuzzi tub.

"What do you think? Do you like it?" He breathed.

I nodded, on the verge of tears. This was the single most sweetest thing anyone has ever done for me.

"You really did this for me?"

"All for you," he nodded. "I thought you could use a little more pampering. And now," he leaned against the jacuzzi tub, "you don't even have to leave the house for it."

"This is amazing."

Tripp's smile grew. "I'm glad you love it. But," he snapped his fingers, "this isn't all."

"More?"

What more could he possibly do for me? He's done so much already.

Taking my hand, he lovingly led me across the hall where his home office and storage room are located. We came to a stop in front of the storage room.

"Open it," he nodded.

Excitedly, I placed my hand on the doorknob.

Tripp sucked in a deep, nervous sounding breath.

I opened up the door, and my own breath caught at the sight.

His storage room, which once housed box after box and stacks of totes filled with various items, had been transformed into the most beautiful, fully stocked nursery.

The walls were painted a light blue, with soft, fluffy clouds hanging from the ceiling. Matching cloud-shaped area rugs were placed underneath the crib and at the foot of the comfortable looking rocking chair in the corner of the room.

A small dresser was filled with tiny little clothes and extra blankets and bedding. Next to it was a fully stocked changing station with more diapers than I hoped we would need.

My fingers trailed over everything as I shook my head in disbelief. With tears welling up in my eyes I turned to Tripp, who was standing in the doorway watching my reaction. "Tripp, this is . . . it's perfect. I can't believe you did this. All of it," I said, referring not only to the nursery, but my bathroom transformation, and giving me a job and basically a new chance at life.

Tripp stepped closer to me, wrapping his arms around me. "I did this because both you and the little guy deserve something amazing."

"I already have you."

He held me closer. "That you do. But I wanted to make you feel special. And to know that I love you, and the baby. You both already mean the world to me."

With those words the tears flowed free, and I buried my face in Tripp's chest. "I love you too," was all I could manage to say.

Tripp lightly brushed away the tears with his thumbs. I closed my eyes as he leaned in with a tender kiss. It was a silent promise of the amazing life we were about to start together.

As Tripp held me in his arms, my head resting against his beating heart, I felt a sense of peace and love that I've never felt before.

CHAPTER 8

ripp

I'VE NEVER REALLY CARED to decorate for the holidays, but Sophie insisted. I kept putting it off as long as I could, and now it was Christmas Eve. I went out and bought a ton of decorations and hauled a giant tree up to the apartment.

Right now it stood tall and naked in the living room, next to the windows overlooking the entire city. I bought so many damn lights that you'll be able to see this thing shine while standing on the street halfway across the city.

I smiled as I watched Sophie open up the boxes of ornaments, carefully unwrapping each one. She was giddy and excited, placing each one in its place on the tree, and trying to guess the meaning of each one.

Honestly, I had just bought a bunch of random ornaments, unsure of what she would have wanted. The only thing on my mind while purchasing them was surprising her with them. I did manage to throw in a few that really did have meaning though. I'm not completely heartless.

She picked up the ornament that has 'Baby's First Christmas' engraved on it. Her breath hitched as tears began to form in her eyes.

"Hey," I said softly, gently wrapping my arms around her. "Are you okay?"

She nodded, but her eyes glistened with unshed tears. "I just wish . ."

My heart squeezed. I tightened my hold on her. "I know, honey. I wish he could be here too." Even if it meant I couldn't. I would give anything as long as Sophie was happy.

I just hoped she could be happy with me. Every day my love for her only grew stronger. Being with her was the best thing I've ever done in my life.

Being with her made my life complete.

She made *me* complete.

She was everything I wanted and more.

A sudden sharp intake of breath had my eyes flying open. I looked down at Sophie, concern filling every fiber of me.

"Sophie, are you okay?"

She looked up at me, her eyes widening. "I think the baby's coming."

"Are you. . . are you sure?" I asked, panic surging through me.

You always think you're prepared and will be calm and cool until the actual moment is upon you.

Sophie nodded, wincing as another contraction hit her. "Very sure."

In a blur I grabbed our hospital bag and rushed her to the hospital. I'd be lying if I said I remembered the actual drive there.

All I remember is panic and holding Sophie's hand, trying

my best to comfort her as we flew through the flurry of snowflakes.

A few hours later, just as Christmas Day had begun, the cries of a newborn baby boy filled the room. I stood by Sohoie's side the entire time she had been in labor, never once leaving her side.

And I knew I never would again.

The nurses placed him in his mother's arms, and Sophie burst out in tears of happiness.

"He's beautiful," I said, marveling at the little miracle. Leaning down, I placed a gentle kiss on the top of Sophie's sweaty head. "And you did so good, Soph. I'm proud of you."

Sophie looked up at me, eyes shining with a mix of pure love, happiness, and a hint of sorrow.

"And I have the perfect name," I offered.

Her brows knit together. "Really?"

I nodded. "I think we should name him Ryan."

Tears spilled down her face. "Thank you," she whispered after a moment. "It is perfect."

"So is he. You're not so bad yourself," I joked.

Sophie laughed. She held little Ryan close. "This is the best Christmas ever."

"And he is the greatest gift we could have ever asked for."